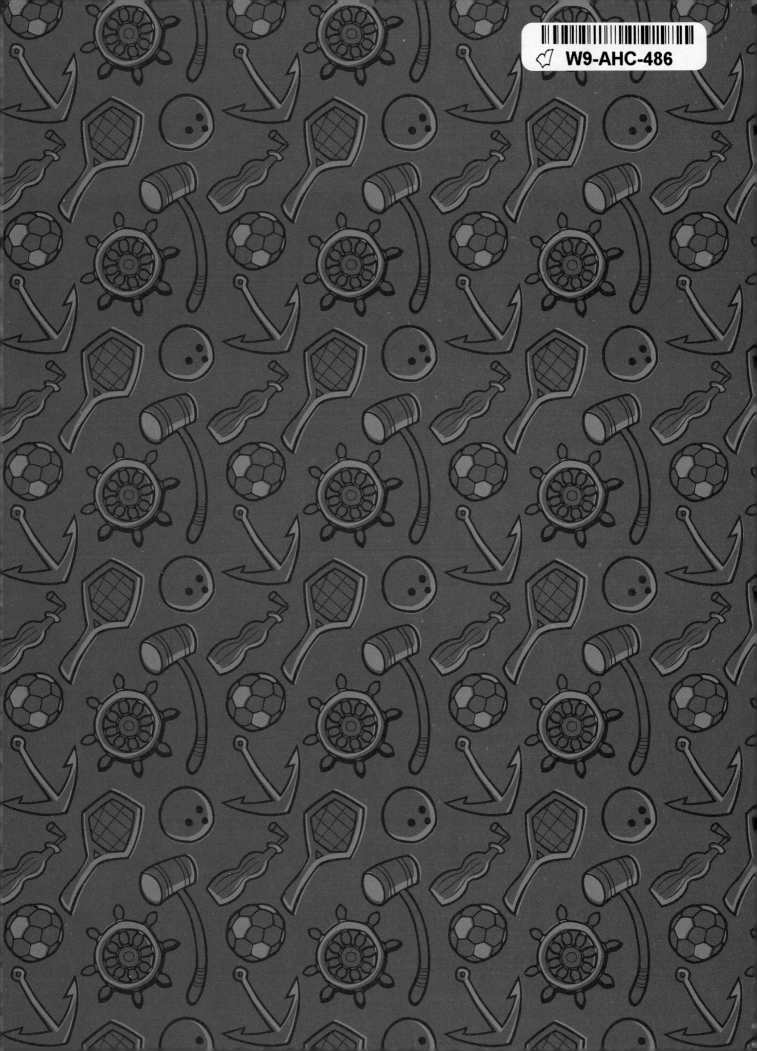

Written by Cindy Kenney

Illustrated by Big Idea Design

Based on the movie: Jonah-a VeggieTales Movie™

Written and Directed by Phil Vischer and Mike Nawrocki

Zonderkidz

www.bigidea.com

Zonder**kidz**™

The children's group of Zondervan
www.zonderkidz.com

Jonah: A Worm's Eye View
Copyright © 2003 by Big Idea Productions, Inc.

Requests for information should be addressed to:
Zondervan: Grand Rapids, Michigan 49530

ISBN: 0-310-70469-3

Written by: Cindy Kenney
Editors: Cindy Kenney and Gwen Ellis
Cover and Interior Illustrations: Greg Hardin and Robert Vann
Cover Design and Art Direction: Karen Poth

Printed in U.S.A.
03 04 05 06 /WP/ 5 4 3 2 1

Hello, my friends!

Have I got a whale of a tale for you! But first, let me introduce myself. My name is Khalil, and I am a worm.

Some worms are slimy. Some worms are tall.
Some worms are silly but fun for all!

Some worms are slippery. Some worms can wiggle.
Some worms tell jokes that can make you giggle!

Some worms are skinny. Some worms are fat,
But why am I just carrying on about that?

Because I am a very special worm! You see, I have a story to share. Have you ever heard a story told from a worm's eye view? Probably not. So I hope this will be a real treat for you!

I want to tell you about a prophet named Jonah. Prophets were a little like mailmen. God used them to deliver very special messages to his people. Jonah became my traveling buddy. But I'm getting ahead of myself.

One dark starry night in Joppa,

Jonah prayed to God. And God answered with a message that Jonah did not expect. God told Jonah to go to a place called Nineveh, but Jonah did not want to go there. The people there lied! They stole! And worst of all, they slapped each other with fishes!

Jonah thought that perhaps God had never been to Nineveh. After all, why would God want to go to a place like that? It was preposterous! So the very next day, Jonah decided to go as far away from Nineveh as possible ... in the opposite direction. I'll go to Tarshish, Jonah thought.

No one wanted to go to such a faraway place. But Jonah spotted a group of very lazy pirates. They were called The Pirates Who Don't Do Anything because they did not do anything ... ever!

These pirates were silly. These pirates were crazy.
These pirates were quite unbelievably lazy!

These pirates ate snacks. These pirates played games.
These pirates were known by their do-nothing claims!

One wore an eye patch, And one wore a hat.
But why am I telling you all about that?

And, of course, these pirates didn't want to go to Tarshish ... until Jonah happened to mention that money was no object. Then they had visions of root beer and cheese curls dancing in their heads. It wasn't long before they were calling out, "I'll hoist the mainsail!" "I'll pop the popcorn!" "I'll get the moist towelettes!"

On that boat is where I met Jonah. He had gone below deck to get some rest and laid his head on a bag of Mister Twisty's Twisted Cheese Curls, a yummy snack food bag in which I had made myself most comfortable. When I realized he was Jonah, the most famous prophet in the whole world, I got so excited! He was a big shot! He was a man God could count on to deliver his messages!

But that day, he was a bit of a grumpy-pants.

Some folks are cheerful. Some folks are mean.
Some folks are sort of right in between.

Some folks are lazy. Some folks are busy.
Some folks have hair that is frightfully frizzy!

Some folks have puppies. Some folks have cats.
But how did I get so off track just like that?

Pretty soon one of the pirates came below the deck to wake Jonah from his nap.

"We seem to have sprung a leak, traveling buddy," I told him calmly as I floated by.

"How can you sleep at a time like this?" the pirate bellowed. "We'll all be fish food if I don't get some help. We're in a storm—like I've never seen before!"

We scrambled onto the deck. **Crash!** went the thunder. **Crack!** went the lightning. **Roar!** went the wind. It was a doozy of a storm!

"Hey! I've got an idea!" said the captain when he spied his friends playing a game of Go Fish. "Somebody up there must be really upset with somebody down here! And it's not gonna let up until we know who that somebody is!" he said. "Shuffle the cards and deal us all in. Loser takes a swim!"

We played that game of Go Fish until everyone was out of the game, except for Jonah and me! Now no one thought Jonah was the reason for the storm. But then Jonah lost the game.

"Alright! I admit it!" Jonah said, startling every one of us! "It's all my fault. I'm the one to blame!"

My new traveling buddy was the cause of that terrible storm!

"I'm running away from God! He told me to go to Nineveh, but I didn't listen. You know, I don't like those people! So I ran and I ended up here, and now everyone's in terrible danger all because of me. I'm afraid the only thing you can do is to throw me into the sea, so it will become calm again!" Jonah wailed.

But one of the pirates had a better idea! "We have a plank," he told us. "You can just walk off!"

So **Kersplash!** That's just what happened.

As soon as Jonah hit the water,

the storm stopped! Everyone cheered. Everyone but Jonah. He started yelling, "Something's touching me!"

We tried frantically to pull him back in. And then the largest fish I have ever seen jumped right up out of the water and swallowed Jonah whole!

Some fish are large. Some fish are small.
Most fish don't like to dance in the fall.

Some fish swim forward. Some fish swim back.
Most fish respond to a delicious worm snack.

Some fish are quiet. Some like to chat.
But why am I talking about all of that?

Especially at a time like this! It was a very tense moment.

"Man the cannon!" one of the pirates shouted, and before long, they were shooting all sorts of things at the fish. Tennis rackets! Croquet mallets! A bowling ball! And I was in it!

"I'm coming, traveling buddy!" I called to Jonah as I sailed through the air.

That's when that big old fish took one more giant gulp and swallowed the bowling ball ... with me still inside it!

Roll, roll, roll. That bowling ball rolled right up to where Jonah was sitting and pouting inside that big fish.

"Oh look, a bowling ball," Jonah said. "If only I could find some pins."

That's when ... "Ta da!" I popped out of the ball. "You found better than that!"

Jonah did not seem a bit pleased to see me. In fact, he was being a big old grumpy-pants. You see, the big difference between Jonah and me was that Jonah saw the whale as half empty ... and I saw the whale as half full!

So Jonah started to pray, "I'm sorry," he told God. "I was wrong." And while he was praying, we heard the most amazing thing! It sounded like singing!

Some songs are needed. Some songs, requested.
This song's about Jonah, a prophet digested.

Some songs teach lessons. Some songs, enhance.
This song involved a strange circumstance.

Some songs flow sweetly. Some songs go flat.
This song was special. Wanna hear about that?

This song told about God being a God of second chances! It gave Jonah hope!

RUMBLE! "What was that?"

GRUMBLE! "I know I heard something!"

RUMBLE, RUMBLE, GRUMBLE, GRUMBLE! It was the fish!

He had big-time indigestion! Then ...

The fish spit us out! We shot through the air like a bullet! We sailed into the sky like an airplane! We were launched from the depths of the sea and the belly of a fish right onto dry land! **OOOF!**

Jonah spit the sand out of his mouth and wiped the seaweed from his eyes. Then he looked up and was delighted to see his trusty camel, Reginald. We climbed right onto Reginald's back and started for Nineveh.

CLIP CLOP. CLIP CLOP. CLIP CLOP.

It was a long journey.

The sky was cloudy and gray when we got to the city. A sign read,

Welcome to Nineveh–
Home of Mister Twisty's Twisted Cheese Curls.

There was another sign too. It read,

Visitors Welcome–to Leave!

And we could hear SLAP! SLAP! SLAP! People were being slapped with fishes!

At the entrance of the city, the guards stopped us. They wouldn't even let us in!

"Well, I tried!" Jonah said and turned around to head for home. But you'll never guess whom we saw! It was our friends from the ship, The Pirates Who Don't Do Anything!

The pirates had taken all the money Jonah had paid them and headed straight to the nearest cheese-curl stand. In bag number 497, they had found the golden ticket! They had won the Mister Twisty's Twisted Cheese Curl Sweepstakes. They had become instant celebrities in Nineveh! So they got us into the city.

We went through the city gates,

and we couldn't believe our eyes! The people there were mean! The people there really did slap each other with fishes!

The people were nasty.
The people did wrong.
The people were naughty
and mean all day long!

The people were loud.
The people were vicious.
The people slapped others
with big slimy fishes!

The people, they screamed.
The people, they spat.
But why am I talking
about all of that?

Especially when something much more important happened to my traveling buddy and me! The city officials came up to us and accused us of high thievery against the royal city of Nineveh! Then they pulled off Pirate Larry's hat, and out fell bags of Mister Twisty's Cheese Curls!

"Wait!" Larry protested. "I thought they were free samples!" But it was too late. **SMACK!** We were all slapped with fishes, and everything went black.

When we woke up, we were tied up! A contraption called The Slap of No Return was in front of us. The thought of it still makes me shiver all the way down to my tail. They put a pumpkin onto the contraption's platform to show us how it worked. Then SWOOSH! A big fish came through the air and splattered that pumpkin into pulp!

"Aaaaaaah!" Jonah and the pirates started crying and blubbering like babies. King Twistomer came out to watch us receive our punishment. "Slap them!" he bellowed.

But my traveling buddy spoke up right before they were about to do it! Jonah told them about our trip inside the belly of the big fish. He explained how he had prayed to God and the monster fish spit us out. But the King was not quite sure if he could believe such an incredible story. So he said, **"Smell them!"**

Let's just say we smelled atrocious!

That's when King Twistomer knew Jonah was telling the truth! The whole city of Nineveh became very quiet. They all settled down to hear Jonah's special message from the Lord.

"STOP IT!" Jonah shouted. That got their attention.

Stop being mean. Stop all your cheating.
Stop all your terrible, nasty fish beating!

Stop all that lying. Stop this bad news.
Stop singing nothing but fish-slapping blues!

Stop doing wrong. Stop being brats.
But after he told them to stop all of that ...

Jonah said, "Especially stop slapping people with fishes! Or this entire city will be destroyed. A message from the Lord!"

Everyone was quite upset. No one had ever told them that they weren't supposed to do that stuff!

The people were sorry. They were sad. So the King signed a decree stating, "Give up your evil ways, and call urgently upon the Lord. Maybe God will give us a second chance!"

Then the King let all of us go free.

Everyone in Nineveh thanked Jonah

for his message and stopped their fish slapping. The sun came back out again, and we bid them all farewell.

After leaving the city, Jonah and I marched to the top of a very big hill. I was not exactly sure what was going on. So I asked Jonah what it was we were doing.

"Oh, it's time to watch the fun!" Jonah told me. "I did what I was supposed to do. I warned them that they were going to get into big trouble. So now it's time to watch God wipe those nasty Ninevites off the face of the Earth!" he gloated.

Some endings are happy. Some endings are sad.
Some endings make people so terribly mad.

Some endings surprise you. Some endings are frightful.
Some endings are wonderfully, simply delightful.

Some endings are peaceful. Some endings KERSPLAT.
But why did I suddenly start with all that?

I'll tell you why! Because this was one ending I did not understand! Jonah thought the bad guys were finally going to get what they deserved.

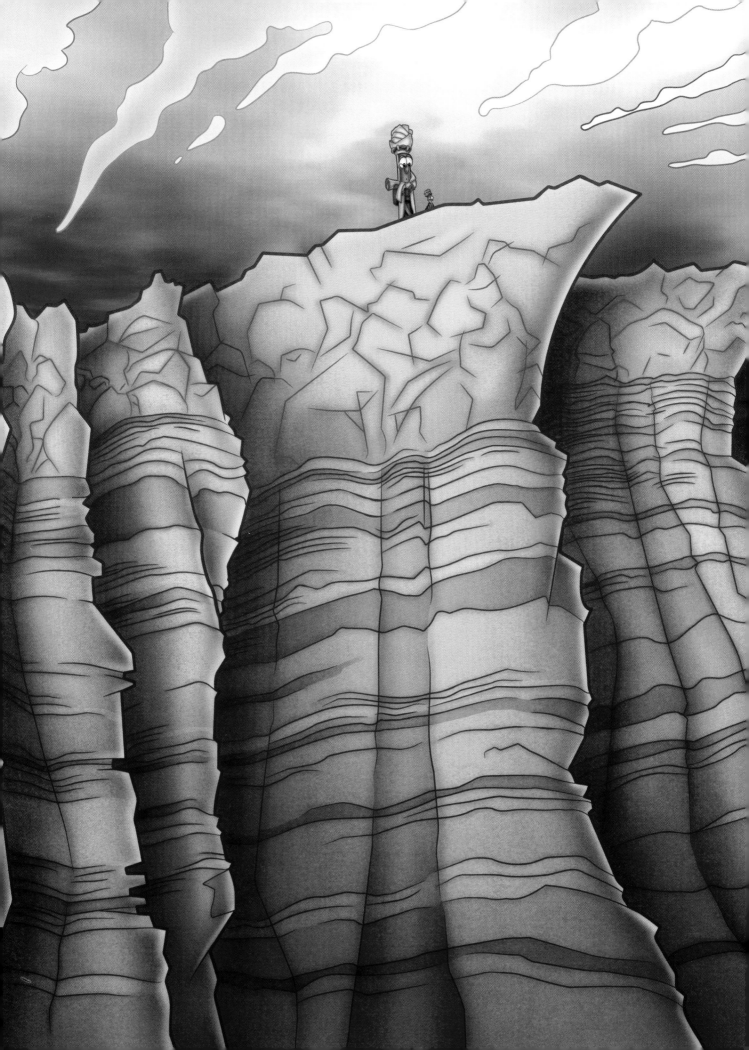

Hours passed. The sun got hotter. Jonah began to wilt in all that heat. But God showed compassion on Jonah once more. He caused a large weed to grow so that Jonah would have shade from the hot sun.

"Oh! Yes! Very nice! Thank you!"
Jonah said.

While Jonah waited for God to punish Nineveh, I got hungry. **CRUNCH! MUNCH!** I began to nibble on that delightfully delicious vine that God had provided. It was oh, so tasty!

Jonah stood up and told God to hurry up with the punishment. Then when he sat back down to lean against his vine ... **CRASH!** Jonah discovered that I had eaten the vine, and he became very angry!

"How could you!" Jonah screeched.

"All your whining made me hungry," I told him. "Besides, it was just a weed."

Then Jonah really lost it! He moaned. He groaned. He wailed. "Just a weed?! It was my shade! It was my friend! Oh, dear Lord, how could you let this happen?"

I couldn't stand it anymore. "Would you look at yourself! You care more about that weed than about all the people of Nineveh! Why are you here now, instead of back in the belly of that big fish?"

Jonah stuttered a bit, then stopped.

"I'll tell you why! Because God is compassionate! And he is merciful! He gave you a second chance. Has it ever occurred to you that maybe God loves everybody? That maybe he wants to give everyone a second chance?"

All Jonah did was sulk. "Oh, I wish I were back in that whale!" he cried.

So I left.

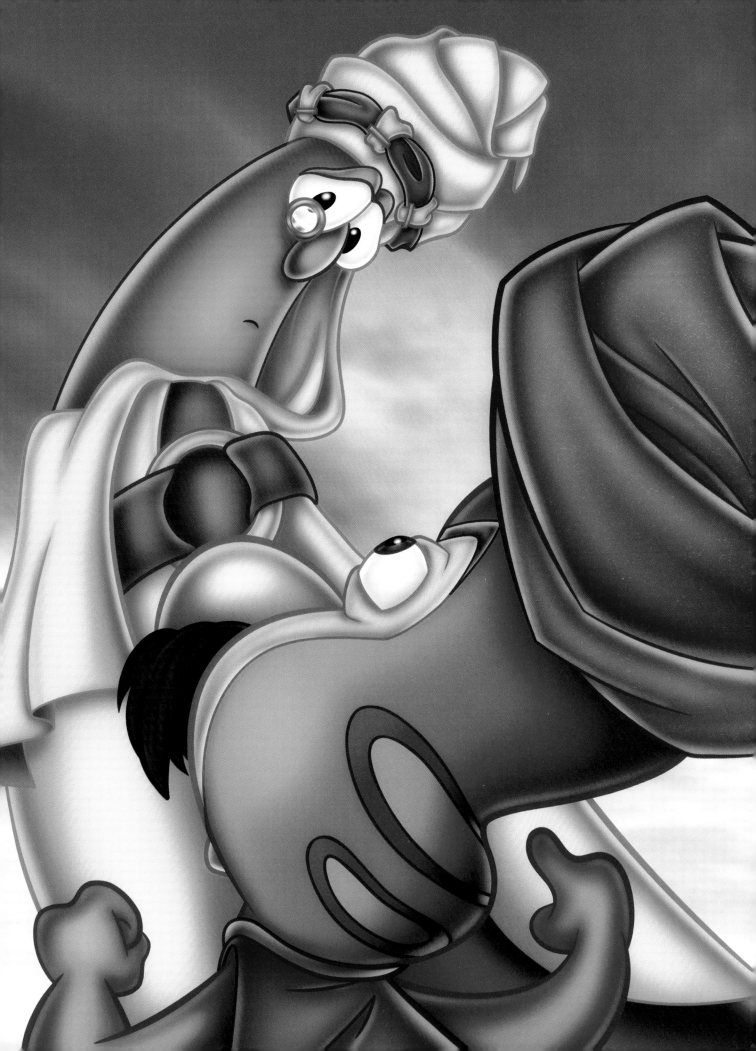

Jonah just didn't get it.

But what about you? Do you understand about second chances?

Some chances are scary. Some chances are fun.
Second chances are offered to anyone.

Some chances inspire. Some chances are clever.
Second chances are giv'n by God forever.

Some chances encourage. Some chances fall flat.
But why all this talk about chances like that?

I will tell you, my friend! Because God offers second chances to everyone! All you have to do is ask! Will you remember to ask God if you need a second chance?

And what about if you need to give someone else a second chance? Will you be a big grumpy-pants? Or will you say: "That's just what I'll do! I want to give others a second chance too!"